How many PIG books have you read? Here are the latest ones. It's best to read them in this order:

7 **PIG** and the Ice-cream Cake

8 **PIG** Skives off School

9 **PIG** is a Blue Baboon's Bottom

10 Super**PIG**!

11 **PIG** and the Baldy Cat

12 **PIG** Leaves Home (for a bit)

13 **PIG** tells a Whopping Great Fib

14 **PIG** is Hairy Snotter

15 **PIG** and the Rainbow Hair

16 **PIG** and the Big Quiz

17 **PIG** gets Angry

18 **PIG**'s Season'

PIG tells a Whopping Great Fib
by Barbara Catchpole
Illustrated by Dynamo

Published by Ransom Publishing Ltd.
Unit 7, Brocklands Farm, West Meon, Hampshire
GU32 1JN, UK
www.ransom.co.uk

ISBN   978 178127 535 1
First published in 2015

PIG

tells a

Whopping
Great Fib

Barbara Catchpole

Illustrated by Dynamo

Ransom

Chips

I'm glad you're here again! I have something important to talk to you about.

I want to talk to you about chips. See, I told you it was important.

I like chips. I like the big soft ones that are at the top. I like the scraggy brown bits too – the ones that have soaked up all the vinegar and get stuck in the corners of the bag.

All I really need to be happy is chips. Definitely not grown-ups! Grown-ups are bonkers – they care about loads of stuff you don't need. I'll tell you about it – hang on – just a bit hungry! [Rustle. Chomp. Lick.]

I was eating chips with Mum, just sitting watching 'Eastenders'. As you do.

Now, Eastenders! There's a programme that shows how bonkers grown-ups are. Everybody's always shouting at each other and getting back at each other. Mum loves it. She shouts at the telly all through it:

'Give him
what for!'

'Don't put up
with it!'

'What did
she do that
for?'

'Get rid of him - waste of space!'

'Look at that blouse she's wearing!'

Anyway, I said to Mum that life seemed very complicated for grown-ups. She said that all 'they' (I think she meant the people in Eastenders-world) - all 'they' needed was some good advice. They needed to be kind to one another.

Then she said her advice to me was to give my wonderful mum the rest of my chips to show her I loved her. In fact, could I pop next door and buy another bag or three?

Problem letters with warts

The next day at school we did problem letters in English. Our normal English teacher had to go back to Canada, so we had a supply teacher with warts and a purple jumper.

When grown-ups get in a mess like on 'Eastenders' - like they murder someone or marry three people at the same time by mistake, they write to a newspaper and then one of the people at the newspaper writes back and gives them advice. It's a proper job – the people who write back are called 'Agony Aunts'.

Anyway, the warty purple-jumper teacher got us to make some of these letters up.

This is mine:

Dear Auntie Pig

I have loads of spots and a big nose and I can't get a girlfriend. What should I do?

From Ugly Raj

Dear Ugly Raj

I think there are loads of things you could do. You could find a girl to take out who is uglier than you (for instance Zoe Zwing) or you could wear a paper bag over your head with holes cut in it (I mean holes cut into the bag, not your head - that wouldn't help). Or you could find a really short-sighted girl and break her glasses before you ask her out.

Good luck! Auntie Pig

Miss said my answers were great and I should get a job doing it when I left school. I did a whole page of them called 'Just Tell Pig'.

Sky Taylor wrote that he was fed up with healthy food and itchy jumpers. I told him to come round our house. He would be glad of the jumper in my bedroom – especially over his pyjamas. It's so cold. And we don't eat anything green at all.

Frankie wrote that he couldn't sleep because all

his little brothers and sisters cried all night. I said he should take our Vampire Baby home for a week.

It wouldn't make any difference, but at least WE would get some sleep and he would 'feel better about himself'. I read that in a magazine: 'feel better about himself'. What a load of rubbish!

The Zwing twins wrote asking who would be the best boyfriend for their sister Zoe. I said get a plastic surgeon. He could fix her face.

I wrote loads! So then I decided to practise on my family and solve all their problems. After all, if it's going to be my job after school, I'll need to get some practice somehow. And my family are all nuts.

Gran on a bike

Santa, Gran's 'boyfriend', looked proper grumpy.

Gran was saying:

> 'I'm just thinking I might do this film
> with Johnny Depp.'

I had been round to Tiff's to play with her
Furby. Do you know about Furbies? They're great!
You can put their
details into your
tablet (I haven't
got one, but if I did)
and make them do a
poo!

Anyway, I couldn't get to play with it. Tiff's
Furby was driving her dad mad and he couldn't
find a tiny screwdriver to take the batteries

out. So he got in a strop and found a hammer
and nails and nailed the toy cupboard shut.

Tiff was crying and you could still hear the
Furby shouting through the door:

'Yoo! Yoo! Yoo!'

I bet he was pooing in the cupboard as he said
that:

'Yoo!' Poo! 'Yoo!' Poo! 'Yoo!' Poo!

Gran's flat is on the way home, so I popped in for a biscuit.

'I might not do it,' she said.

'Too old?'

(I knew what she was talking about).

'No, Johnny's still quite young!'

'I meant you!'

'No, I'm not old! It's just that Johnny's film is bound to have 'young stuff' in it and I haven't got a bike and I haven't been rollerblading for ages. And I said I'd look after Mary's pet while she goes away on her motorbike with Hell's Grannies.'

Santa asked me:

'What shall I do, Pig? I hate it when she goes away.'

I said:

'Just tell me all about it.'

This was a chance to give good advice!

'I can't trim my
own toenails and
I can't see in my
own ears to cut
my ear hair! I
can't cope!'

I thought about what Mum said about being
kind, so I said to Santa he should let her go. He
could easily look after Mary's pet.

Gran was delighted. She said:

> 'Oh that's great! She can bring Snappy
> round to you – I expect one bath is much
> the same as another to a baby alligator!'

Santa looked even more hacked off.

Schrödinger's Gran

I told Mum about Gran and the film.

Mum laughed and told me about a scientist called
Schrödinger (She said it like 'Shrow-ding-er').
I think he was a proper
nutty professor with mad
hair and a German accent,
like in the cartoons.

Anyway, he bunged a cat in a box and what he said was, while he didn't look in the box, the cat was both dead and not dead. (Like a zombie, maybe?) The cat was only one or the other if you looked.

I thought a lot about this while I ate my pork chop, chips and beans. I reckon it's mental. Leave a cat in a box for days and it'll be alive

for a while, then it'll die. Ask any cat (unless it's been in a box for too long). I reckon someone should have told the RSPCA.

I got upset and, like always happens, I could feel a huge fart building up inside me. Or it may have been the beans. Mum was still talking, so I held it in. It might go away. You never know.

Mum carried on:

'Anyway, that's what I reckon about Gran. She might be friends with Johnny Depp, or she might be an old lying liar. While I

don't know, I don't care. She is sort of
both of those things. Schrödinger's Gran!
Oh, Pig, that is disgusting! Is that you?
Phew!'

Schrödinger's fart

I explained:

'I didn't know if I could keep it in or not.'

'Schrödinger's fart!'

My mum laughed, but she still
made me stand in the back
yard by the pile of rocks until
the smell went away. That
fart was definitely alive.

Suki dumps Kim

Wallop! Suki slammed the
front door.

She yelled at Mum:

'Don't you dare let him
in! I'm never
talking to him
again! The rat!'

Mum said:

'Hello, Suki! Nice to see you too!'

What had Kim done? Turns out he drove Suki to
a modelling job – a magazine advert for
chicken nuggets. Now the lady said Suki wasn't

right for the job (probably because she looks like she's not eaten anything all her life, not ever, let alone chicken nuggets) but the lady liked the look of Kim.

Suki said:

'She liked the look of him alright. Oh yes, and I think he liked the look of her!'

Anyway, they took
loads of pictures of
Kim and gave him a
hundred quid. Suki had
to wait around all day.
She was really cross.
Spitting feathers!

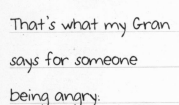

That's what my Gran
says for someone
being angry:

    'She was spitting feathers!'

I asked Mum:

    'What should he have done?'

Mum said:

'I know the answer to that. Kim should have turned down the job without looking at the pretty lady, keeping his eyes on the floor all the time, and taken Suki shopping to cheer her up. Of course. Shame! I quite liked Kim. Still, he might get back with Suki.'

I could hear Kim shouting through the front door. He was like a giant Furby shut in a toy cupboard.

Kim tried (really)

The next day Kim brought some flowers round for Suki.

'How nice!'

said Suki and threw them in the bin.

The next day he sent chocolates. Mum whipped those off the bloke quickly and we sat and watched 'The Terminator' that evening and she pigged them. I had a bag of sweet eyeballs.

I sat up until eleven, even though it was a school night. Result!

The next day, Kim was waiting for me when I came home from school. I told him Mum had eaten the chocolates.

He asked:

'What shall I do, Pig? You know her better than anyone. Help me!'

I said:

'Just tell me all about it.'

I was going to give him really good advice.

I saw this film once where the bloke stood under the girl's bedroom window and sang to her. Then she fell in love with him and it was all great.

If that didn't work, he would have to buy her something that cost shed-loads of money.

Kim said he only knew Elvis songs, so I said not

to do 'Hound Dog' or 'Blue Suede Shoes' (I think
I've spelled that right).

That night Kim sang 'The Wonder of You' on
the pavement outside our house. The nice Polish
lady who lives above the chip shop threw

potatoes at him.
Then Suki got
him with a
bucket of water.
She forgot to
hold onto the
bucket, but it
was only a plastic
one. Still, bet it
hurt.

One of the potatoes cut Kim's eye and Mum had to call an ambulance.

The next day Suki told me to paint her toenails and I said:

'In your dreams.'

So she painted her own. That was when we knew Kim was properly dumped. She didn't text him and make him come round and do it.

Mum went out and collected the potatoes in the plastic bucket and made chips, but I think she was a bit sad.

Bob and the barmaid

I haven't talked about Bob yet. THAT Bob - you know, Mum's 'boyfriend'. (BOYfriend! Ha Ha!). Anyway, this bit's about him.

Raj stupidly left his specs just on the bit of his bed where I bounce, so he had to go into town to collect new ones.

'I saw him, Pig! I saw him!'

This was Raj. He phoned me from the High Street, all excited.

'He was outside the spare gold shop and he

was getting into it with Tish, the barmaid from the Slug and Lettuce – the one with the pink hair and the mole!'

'Into it? Who? What? I don't understand.' I didn't understand.

'Not 'into it'. Intimate! Bob! Your mum's boyfriend was kissing Tish with the pink hair and the mole.'

'Bob?'

'Yes! Bob!'

I think I knew what Raj was telling me.

The lies

So what should I do? I had to get rid of Bob
the Love Rat. That's what.

To be honest, Bob looked too
boring to be a Love Rat.
More like a Love Sheep, but
what did I know? I cared a
lot about Mum and I didn't
want her hurt.

I could advise her to dump him, but she wouldn't do it! She knew I wanted her to get back together with Dad and take me to live in his beach bar in Spain where I could go in the sea all day.

You don't have to go to school in Spain at all! Not ever. I read it on the internet somewhere.

This was not a time for advice – it was a time for action! I was good at sorting out grown-ups' lives!

I went round to Bob's. I had to be cruel. It had to be done. I owed it to Mum (and Spain did look lovely on the internet). I played with

Baldy Cat and fed her a biscuit while I talked.

I couldn't look Bob in the eyes.

'Mum says she can't go out with you
tomorrow.'

'But we were going to the Slug and
Lettuce!'

I bet you were, I thought. To see the pink hairy moley lady.

I said:

'Well now you can't. Tomorrow I think she's seeing that bloke with the big red sports car. He can't park it down our street — it's so big. I think they are going to listen to jazz together, or maybe go skiing.'

Bob stared at me with his mouth open.

'Or it might be the bloke she sees on Tuesdays when she tells you she is washing her hair. They go clubbing down the

Ibiza-a-go-go in Canal Street. He's a lot
younger than you are and very fit. We're
all going on a holiday together – to Spain!'

Bob made a funny noise and sat on his white
leather sofa with his head in his hands (I don't
mean his head came off. Gross! His head was
still attached to his neck. Just to be clear.)

Baldy Cat sat next
to him and coughed
up a fur ball. I
don't think biscuits
are good for her.

Now for the killer blow!

'Or it might be the film director that Gran knows. He wants to put Mum in a film. He does so much exciting stuff – surfing and stuff. He has his own plane. He said he wanted to go out with Mum because ... because ... because he likes chips!'

My work was done. Bob was a broken man. He was crying. What a wuss! Serves him right for getting into it with Miss Mole!

Ooops!

It was Wednesday night.

Mum said:

'I can't understand where Bob has got to.

We were going to the Slug and Lettuce
with his brother and his new girlfriend,
that barmaid with the pink hair.'

What? Bob was kissing his brother's girlfriend!
I knew that wasn't good.

'Do you know, Pig? Bob's brother looks just
like Bob. They could be twins!'

 I said nothing. After that, I said a bit more nothing. I could feel a fart, deep inside, trying to escape.

I had made a humongous mistake! Well, to be fair, Raj had made a humongous mistake! Again! Bob was innocent.

I had to get to Bob before ...

Suddenly Mum's face lit up.

'Oh, I've had a text from Bob! I'll just see what he says!'

She read the text and made a little noise.

'Oh! Oh!'

She sat down suddenly.
She put the phone down
and a huge tear plopped
down on the table next
to it. Another fell into

the hamster cage, right onto Harry's head. He

woke up and looked puzzled. It rolled off his

nose in a big drip.

It was for the best. Now there would be no

more boring Bob the bossy boyfriend. Mum

might even phone Dad in Spain. Or I could

phone him.

Mum said:

'Come and give me a hug.'

She was crying properly now, like only girls can cry: you know – making loads of noise when they breathe in. Harry went and sheltered in his toilet. It was like a monsoon in there!

I said:

'Not now. I've got to phone someone. Straight away.'

What should I do?

Help me! Help me! What should I do? What COULD I do?

Number one plan:

    I could phone Dad and ask him to come home or let us come to Spain. I could tell him how Mum had got dumped – I knew she wouldn't mind me telling him. I could rely on Dad to make it alright.

Number two plan:

    I could tell Bob I lied to him and we could be back to Boring 'Only take one biscuit,' 'Have you done your homework?' 'It's about your bedtime,' Bob – bobbing about the

house in his horrible
Swedish detective
jumpers. Then I
thought about Mum
crying.

I didn't have much choice,

did I?

Thirty minutes later

I was sat on the sofa watching the show.

The woman was saying:

'So let me get this right. You believed that

I was going out with three different

blokes, just because some idiot told you it

was true! You then dumped me by text! By text!'

'I am so sorry, I don't know what I was thinking! I love you so much. I just can't believe you want to go out with me! Please forgive me!'

No! This wasn't 'Eastenders'! It was the Bob and Susan Show. (No, I don't know why she wants to go out with him either).

So you're right - it was plan number two. I'd

phoned Bob, not my Dad. I just couldn't let Mum get upset.

Then I just sat and watched:

1) Santa rushed in asking what alligators eat, apart from fingers.

2) Suki rushed in asking Bob to teach her how to drive because Kim was going to buy her a car. (Idiot. Idiots. Both of them. And Bob too, if he says 'yes'.)

3) Gran phoned to say she needed us to send any spare money for her to have parachuting lessons.

4) The nice Polish lady came in shouting about potato thieves.

5) Bob's brother and Hairy Pink Mole Lady rushed in asking where Bob was. Hairy Pink Mole Lady sat down to watch 'Eastenders' with me.

6) Harry pushed all his wet bedding out of his cage in a strop.

7) Mum and Bob smiled at each other and held hands.

I tell you, this was better than Eastenders, any day. I don't know why we bother with a telly.

But I'm not going to be an Agony Aunt any more. Nobody could help my family!

Three more things I don't quite get:

1) What is 'spare money'?

2) I bet Gran isn't as good at parachuting as Johnny Depp. The falling bit is easy. The hard bit is landing AND staying alive AND not breaking your legs. Johnny Depp's got to better than Gran at that bit.

3)   Bob ruffled my hair and said:

'I won't forget this, Pig.'

He was smiling, but I am a bit worried. What will he do to get his own back?

The next **PIG** book is

PIG

is

Hairy Snotter

About the author

Barbara Catchpole was a teacher for thirty years and enjoyed every minute. She has three sons of her own who were always perfectly behaved and never gave her a second of worry.

Barbara also tells lies.